The Library of Souls

A COLLECTION OF TEN HORROR SCRIPTS, TALES, AND POEMS

THE LIBRARY OF SOULS:
A COLLECTION OF TEN HORROR SCRIPTS, TALES, AND POEMS

By Andrew Buckner

The Library of Souls: A Collection of Ten Horror
Scripts, Tales and Poems

Copyright © 2024 Andrew Buckner
Published by Requiem Press.

Cover image Vecteezy.com

A Requiem Press book.

ISBN: 979-8-9899561-1-1

TABLE OF CONTENTS

SCRIPTS

PROSE TALES

POETRY TALES

WRITING PROMPT

ABOUT THE AUTHOR **95**

ACKNOWLEDGMENTS

The following collection is dedicated to my wife, Valerie, my mom, Pamela, and my two daughters, Bianca and Arianna, whose love and support keeps the pen moving on the page.

DEAD AIR!

FADE IN:

INT. A SEEMINGLY ABANDONED LIVING ROOM - NIGHT

A TURNED OFF TELEVISION IS SEEN IN CLOSE-UP IN THE MIDDLE OF A PITCH BLACK, SEEMINGLY ABANDONED LIVING ROOM.

An analog clock hovering just above the television hits midnight.

As soon as the clock hits this time, the television turns itself on.

INT. INSIDE THE TELEVISION SET - SAME TIME

A long-beloved horror host in his late seventies, JEREMIAH "THE SCHLOCKMEISTER" BOGGINS, is seen on the television about to begin his 3-day marathon of all types of terror films, which is simply titled THE HORROR-A-THON.

BOGGINS is seen on the television screen in a bloody apron with a hatchet sticking out of his head. He is smiling happily and cooking something on the stove. This is in an act to make him appear like the cannibal killer, THE NECKER, in the movie he is about to host.

> BOGGINS
> (to the audience, on-screen)
> Welcome, horror fiends! I'm JEREMIAH "THE SCHLOCKMEISTER" BOGGINS! We'll now be starting our 72-hour horror movie marathon, imaginatively titled by the fine

folks at BLOODTHIRST STREAMING as THE
HORROR-A-THON.

Our goal with this marathon is to show
one film from as many horror sub-genres
as we can cover in a 3-day time frame.

We are starting all of this off with the
once thought to be lost, low-budget,
1980's slasher film, KNIFE TO THE NECK!

Now, what I'm doing here is…

BOGGINS flips the skillet he is using.

THE AUDIENCE GETS A GLIMPSE OF THE MEATY
SUBSTANCE, WHICH IS OOZING PINK SLIME, THAT HE
IS COOKING.

A gagging sound is heard from one of the crew
members on-screen.

            BOGGINS
        (continued)
…preparing a meal our cannibal villain in
the upcoming film, who is simply known as
"THE NECKER", would approve of. It's the
flesh of some of our crew members, I
won't say whom, that wouldn't cater to my
every whim.

And we all know what happens when I don't
get my every whim catered to.

> You see, when I say I need all the red
> M&MS out of my candy jar in my trailer, I
> mean it! This ain't a game!

BOGGINS chuckles to himself.

> BOGGINS
> (continued)
> Maybe one day they will understand what
> serious business this is!

A laugh track is heard from BOGGINS' remark.

BOGGINS addresses one of the crew members of
the marathon who is off-screen.

> BOGGINS
> Andrew, could you bring up a picture of
> our good pal, THE NECKER, for our fine
> viewers, please?

A picture of THE NECKER, a hefty man in the
same bloody apron BOGGINS is wearing and
carrying a hatchet in one hand like BOGGINS
has in his head and a butcher knife in the
other, flashes on-screen.

INT. A SEEMINGLY ABANDONED ROOM - A MOMENT LATER

An overweight, middle-aged man, UMBERTO
LEONARDO, who is in his early forties, is
ravenously drinking beer and eating popcorn in
a reclining chair.

A flash of lightning reveals THE NECKER
standing behind UMBERTO with a butcher knife
just inches away from his neck.

UMBERTO remains unaware of the danger he is in as he spills popcorn and beer all over himself and the recliner while frantically consuming them both.

>   BOGGINS
>   (O.S.)
> Now, I'm sure my highly educated fellow film fanatics out there will recall that THE NECKER was given his nickname because of his signature kill style. He slits the throat of his victims with the butcher knife he carries in his right hand, then he scalps them with the ax he car-ries in his left hand. Afterward, he will make a meal of them and eat their brains for dinner.

While BOGGINS is heard making these statements about THE NECKER, THE NECKER is doing the things BOGGINS says to UMBERTO while BOGGINS is saying them.

THE NECKER stands in front of UMBERTO, who is slumped over dead after THE NECKER finishes the kill routine BOGGINS just mentioned, and sticks a straw in his open brain cavity.

An exaggerated slurping sound is heard as THE NECKER drinks the fluids from UMBERTO's head via the straw.

BOGGINS speaks off-screen after THE NECKER is done drinking as if THE NECKER's actions triggered a bit of information BOGGINS had forgotten.

                    BOGGINS
                (O.S.)
            Oh, yeah, I must've forgotten!

            THE NECKER always carries a straw on him
            for those stubborn brain juices of his
            victims he can't quite get to on his own.

            Where does he carry it? Nobody knows.
            Maybe in his own brain.

The same laugh track from before is heard
again.

THE NECKER, still drinking brains from a
straw, turns his head and smiles sinisterly as
he watches BOGGINS.

After a moment, BOGGINS takes the beer from
UMBERTO's hand and puts the remaining contents
into UMBERTO's skull cavity.

THE NECKER greedily slurps this up with his
straw, while snacking on UMBERTO's popcorn.

BEGIN TITLES.

TITLE CARD: *DEAD AIR!*

END TITLES.

**<u>INT. THE OFFICES OF BLOODTHIRST STREAMING - A
FEW MINUTES LATER</u>**

FREDERICK BATEMAN, The CEO of BLOODTHIRST
STREAMING is pacing a meeting room in THE
OFFICES OF BLOODTHIRST STREAMING. He is
screaming at someone on his cell phone.

> BATEMAN
> (to the person on his phone)
> Pull it off the air! I don't care if it
> will ignite a social media firestorm,
> BLOODTHIRST STREAMING can't use any more
> negative publicity!

BATEMAN waits a moment while the person on the
other end of the phone responds.

> BATEMAN
> (to the person on his phone)
> (continued)
> Look, I'm sure this is just another movie
> nut who has taken his love of BOGGINS and
> scary movies too far! I'm sure he, she,
> it, they, or whom-ever it ends up being,
> will be apprehended soon! But, until that
> time, pull the live stream off the air!
> And that's final!

BATEMAN violently hits a button on his phone
to end his call.

BATEMAN turns to BOGGINS and mutters to
himself before addressing BOGGINS.

> BATEMAN
> (continued)
> (to himself)
> Goddamn horror fans and their goddamn
> horror obsessions!

BOGGINS knows he shouldn't say anything to his
boss, but he makes a joke to lighten the mood
(and because he can't help it).

                    BOGGINS
How dare you speak our lord's name in
vain!

BATEMAN changes his tone a bit and moves
towards BOGGINS, ignoring his latest joke.

                    BATEMAN
What are we going to do, BOGGINS?

We've got twenty-two reported murders,
with more coming in as we speak! From
what I'm hearing, it all happened around
the time you put up THE NECKER's picture
on the live stream.

That means, we have at least twenty-two
NECKER copycats, who are all big fans of
yours, who have decided to imitate this
fictional slasher at the same time and in
the same way!

You know what that means, BOGGINS?

                    BOGGINS
We have a SCREAM-type situation going on?

                    BATEMAN
No! Well, yes, but, no! That means
BLOODTHIRST STREAMING will be no more!
That means more lawsuits and my millions
of viewers and their precious dollars are
going bye-bye right out the digital
window!

                    BOGGINS
Are we sure this couldn't have been done
by one person? I mean, the average

slasher villain has an uncanny ability to
be in numerous places at once. Take the
later FRIDAY THE 13Th sequels for
example…

BATEMAN is closing his eyes in an effort to
calm himself while BOGGINS continues to
blabber.

BATEMAN begins rubbing his temples as a
headache forms from listening to BOGGINS.

          BATEMAN
This is not a movie, BOGGINS!

          BOGGINS
No, but since THE NECKER is movie-based
it should, theoretically, follow similar
logic.

          BATEMAN
You know what? Even if your theory is
correct, the HORROR-A-THON still resulted
in multiple murders! That's our bottom
line!

That still means my neck is going to be,
as they say in Hollywood, severed by the
media guillotine.

          BOGGINS
Nobody says that. They never have and
they never will.

Not to mention, I, personally, don't
believe that it is a fan of mine or of
horror, or both, doing this.

Horror, contrary to popular opinion, actually creates empathy. It's a safe way for anxious, fearful people to explore their fears in a safe space. That is why so many, shall we say, outcasts and anti-socialites love and crave it so much.

It isn't, as the antiquated stereotype for us horrorphiles goes, that we are violent people who revel in the violence and brutality on-screen.

You see, the catharsis isn't so much in the bloodshed on-screen, though we do love that, but in the safety of the scare.

    BATEMAN
   (turning away from BOGGINS)
Fine. That's really neither here nor there, but that's fine.

We're still pulling the plug on the live stream.

BATEMAN's cell phone rings. He answers it.

    BATEMAN
   (to the person on the other end of his phone)
This is Bateman!

BATEMAN listens.

                    BATEMAN
               (continued)
          How? Are we sure the live stream was
          pulled from all devices? Does the live
          stream still show on the television and
          not on the phone app? I've only tried it
          on the phone app!

BATEMAN listens.

                    BATEMAN
               (continued)
          Then how are these murders still
          occuring?

BATEMAN listens.

                    BATEMAN
               (continued)
          Okay. We're sending BOGGINS in.

BATEMAN ends the call. He turns to BOGGINS.

                    BATEMAN
          We're up to 40 murders! The live stream
          was pulled twenty minutes ago, but, alas,
          the murders still continue!

          So, how is this not an obsessed fan? Who
          else would know these movies so
          intricately that they can keep up with
          what is going on in the film as it occurs
          during the live stream without actually
          seeing it unfold?

BOGGINS considers this question and is quiet
for a moment.

                    BOGGINS
                (to BATEMAN)
                (continued)
Aliens are usually a good scapegoat in
these types of stories! Or good, old-
fashioned evil technology! Or, maybe
brainwashing! Like, a cult-type scenario.

Maybe the demon of a recently executed
serial killer is loose in the wires of
our TVs and is playing these films
without our consent somehow in order to
cause this bloodshed as an act of
maniacal vengeance to those who sent him
to the electric chair.

Or, maybe we should just wait and see if
the villain of the next film makes an
appearance, before we do something rash,
like interrupt the live stream with a
live stream that is, gasp, unscripted
and, gasp part two, actually live!

                    BATEMAN   ·
                (even angrier)
                And risk more bodies on *my* watch
                because *I* didn't take prompt action?
                Never.

But, after BATEMAN says this, he stops and
thinks for a moment.

                    BATEMAN
                (continued)
                    (to BOGGINS)
                Who or what is our next villain?

                    BOGGINS
A giant mosquito.

                    BATEMAN
Son of a bitch!

                    BOGGINS
Indeed! You know that is actually a
few letters changed and removed from
the original tagline for the film,
"Son of an itch"! That is, at least
in its more daring 1981 Italian
releases.

You see, PROBOSCIS is the heart-
warming story of a scientist who
can't stop itching after being
bitten by a forty-foot, once thought
to be long dead prehistoric mosquito
while doing research on human
transformation in the rain forests
of the Amazon jungle.

As he scratches, the mark gets
bigger and bigger. He tries to do
experiments to get the bite to
decrease. That is, until one night
when his son, ZACHARIAH FULLSTEIN,
accidentally mistakes the serum for
his night-night juice, in adult
human talk: milk, and turns into a
forty-foot mosquito that flies all
over the world to kill random people
and suck their blood in order to
survive.

Spoiler alert: ZACHARIAH's dad ends
up realizing that his serum only

                    13

makes his bite grow. He doesn't
recognize this until the bite gets
so big that he can't walk or move
and eventually he just explodes into
a big mass of yellow puss.

It's really a great practical
effect! You have to see it!
Spoiler alert 2 - Electric Boogaloo:
ZACHARIAH ends up suffering the same
fate as his dad. But, not until he
attacks every major city, a la
GODZILLA.

    BATEMAN
   (with an almost comical look on
   his face)
Thanks, Boggins. That was convoluted
and unnecessary but, uh, fascinating.

It really filled in a lot of gaps in
the exposition of our little tale
here.

BATEMAN's tone changes back to anger after he
winks at the audience.

    BATEMAN
   (continued)
I wonder how many more people have
been killed while you were blab-
bering about "boogaloos".

BATEMAN's tone changes to less angry, but
still stern because it is the only way to ask
BOGGINS to do what BATEMAN wants him to do.

                    BATEMAN
                (continued)
          What I need you to do is take your
          wide-reaching knowledge of horror
          live on the channel and use it to
          solve these murders!

BATEMAN's tone changes again.

                    BATEMAN
                (continued)
          Did I mention that already?

                    BOGGINS
                (uncertain)
          I believe so.

                    BATEMAN
          Sorry, I haven't slept in about
          fifty-plus years. Plus, my wife is
          leaving me and…

BOGGINS, with no patience for BATEMAN going on
about his personal life the way BOGGINS does
with horror movies, suddenly interrupts
BATEMAN.

                    BOGGINS
          To the 3-day HORROR-A-THON mobile!

A random musical note punctuates BOGGINS' last
statement after he says it.

BATEMAN has a confused look flash over his
face as BOGGINS runs off before BATEMAN can
answer with his arms outstretched in front of
him like a superhero.

BEGIN MONTAGE:

A montage of a mosquito and other various horror villains, such as a giant plant and a killer lunch box that chokes its victims with the straps on its side, slaying random people who are all drinking beer and eating popcorn on their couch in the same position as UMBERTO was in at the beginning of the HORROR-A-THON.

During the montage, BOGGINS is seen, with a subtitle below him on-screen that announces THIS TIME WE ARE ACTUALLY LIVE!, describing the movie that is coming up and the various ways the characters use to kill the villain in the movie in hopes that this will cause potential victims to do the same to the villain when it attacks them.

He does this in hopes of quickly ending the slaughter caused by the HORROR-A-THON.

During the scene that opens this montage, A GIANT BUG flies down from the sky and bites THE MAN sitting on the couch.

He is in the same position as all the other beer drinking and popcorn eating victims of THE HORROR-A-THON.

THE MAN explodes into a pile of yellow puss when the GIANT BUG bites his neck.

After this bit, BOGGINS is heard screaming:

                    BOGGINS
                    (O.S.)
        Get the bug repellent! Get THE RAID!
        Spray, baby, spray!

ANOTHER MAN is seen watching this bit. He
pulls out his BUG REPELLENT after BOGGINS
tells him to do so.

                    ANOTHER MAN
        Locked and loaded, LORD BOGGINS!

ANOTHER MAN sprays the bug as it flies towards
his neck. It does nothing.

ANOTHER MAN also explodes into a bucket of
yellow puss after he tries to spray THE
MOSQUITO and, in turn, THE MOSQUITO bites his
neck.

After ANOTHER MAN explodes, the MOSQUITO sits
down on the couch where ANOTHER MAN was sit-
ting before he exploded.

THE MOSQUITO ravenously consumes his popcorn
and drinks ANOTHER MAN's beer.

In doing so, the MOSQUITO, who is seen with
some yellow puss on its backside sitting where
ANOTHER MAN exploded, grows.

After this, the KILLER LUNCH BOX is seen pop-
ping up from behind a couch and choking AN
ELDERLY WOMAN who is also eating popcorn and
drinking beer.

While this is occurring, BOGGINS is heard
saying:

                    BOGGINS
                    (O.S.)
          …Now "THE BOX", as he is called in
          the film, is killed by being zipped
          shut with crazy glue so its zippered
          teeth can't bite the neck of its
          victims. Which, you will soon see,
          it sure enjoys doing.

          The strap of "THE BOX" was also cut
          off in the movie with scissors, so
          it can't strangle anyone.

          After this is done, the heroine of
          the picture, SUZETTE RILEY (bril-
          liantly played by WIGOURNEY LEAVER),
          stuffs "THE BOX" in her downstairs
          freezer.

          She then keeps her hip on the door
          until it freezes to death, a la the
          finale of STANLEY KUBRICK's immortal
          1980 horror classic, THE SHINING.

The ELDERLY WOMAN, who is still being
strangled and is hunched over and dying with
red eyes from the impact of being choked by
"THE BOX", gasps with her dying breath and
slowly speaks each letter of the following
words as she says:

                    ELDERLY WOMAN
          Hey, spoiler alert!

After saying this, she keels over and dies.

THE BOX pushes THE ELDERLY WOMAN aside, opens up its zipper, and dives headfirst into the popcorn after guzzling THE ELDERLY WOMAN's beer.

In doing so, THE BOX grows to a larger size.

THE BOX's strap also grows bigger. For a moment, it looks like an arm that has gotten stronger and is being flexed by THE BOX in admiration.

BOGGINS is heard in the background for a moment after the lunch box kills ANOTHER WOMAN in her mid-twenties in a HORROR HIGH UNIVERSITY t-shirt.

BOGGINS IS REFLECTED THROUGH THE DEAD WOMAN'S STILL OPEN RIGHT EYE AS THE LUNCH BOX IS HEARD GUZZLING HER BEER AND EATING HER POPCORN.

CUT TO CLOCKS SPINNING FRANTICALLY, AS IF POSSESSED, TO SIGNIFY THE PASSAGE OF TIME.

> BOGGINS
> Okay, so the vampire in this film isn't hurt by light like the average vampire, so our hero, an astronaut, lassoes the sun and…

MORE CLOCKS SPIN FRANTICALLY TO SIGNIFY THE PASSAGE OF TIME.

> BOGGINS
> (continued)
> Okay, our next little monster in the "Little Monsters" segment of our 3-day HORROR-A-THON is a killer baby

and, I don't recommend you do this
to your baby at home, well, maybe
your Aunt Edna's, but it is killed
by…

MORE CLOCKS SPIN AROUND TO SIGNIFY THE PASSAGE
OF TIME.

> BOGGINS
> (continued)
> Now, in our latest "Deadly Animals"
> segment of the 3-day HORROR-A-THON,
> we have a family of deadly cats who
> come together to do the one thing
> that brings all families together,
> kill, in LERGIO SEONE's spaghetti
> western-influenced THE LITTER from
> 1976.
>
> Now, these felines are taken out in
> the film by…

MORE CLOCKS SPIN AROUND TO SIGNIFY THE PASSAGE
OF TIME.

> BOGGINS
> (continued)
> Hey, why are we still showing these
> films? Isn't that the way we
> suggested earlier that might stop
> the killers from these films from
> killing in real life?
>
> Oh, well. I guess there really is
> nothing worse than dead air. Get it?
> Dead air.

A laugh track is heard from somewhere off-screen.

MORE CLOCKS SPIN AROUND TO SIGNIFY THE PASSAGE OF TIME.

BOGGINS looks down at his beer and his bowl of popcorn that he hasn't touched, but uses as a prop in his show for ambiance, and a thought occurs to him.

                    BOGGINS
                 (continued)
          It's the beer and the popcorn: the
          official snack of horrorphiles
          worldwide! Stop drinking it! Stop
          eating it! It's what gives the
          killer kernels in our next feature
          from 1966, which is appropriately
          titled KERNELS!, their strength and
          increased bloodthirst!

A TEENAGE VIEWER HEARS THIS, LOOKS AT THE POPCORN IN HIS FIST THAT IS ABOUT TO GO IN HIS MOUTH, AND RAISES HIS POPCORN-LADEN FIST TO THE TELEVISION.

                    TEENAGE VIEWER
          You can't tell me what to do! This
          is AMERICA, Land of the free and
          home of people named DAVE, or some-
          thing!

With these rebellious words stated, the TEEN-AGE VIEWER downs his fistful of popcorn and immediately begins choking.

THE TEENAGE VIEWER explodes.

KERNELS OF POPCORN roll out of THE TEENAGE
VIEWER's open mouth after he dies, high-five
one another, and run off-screen.

> KERNELS OF POPCORN
> (O.S., in unison)
> We're free! We're free!

CUT TO CLOCKS SPINNING AGAIN IN A FRENZY TO
SIGNIFY THE PASSAGE OF TIME.

ON THIS OCCASION, THE CLOCKS STOP RIGHT AT
MIDNIGHT.

BOGGINS can be heard in the background.

> BOGGINS
> (O.S.)
> Hello, is anyone still alive out
> there?

CUT TO VARIOUS DEAD BODIES, ALL HORROR-A-THON
VIEWERS, WITH BEER AND POPCORN SPILLED ALL
OVER THEM.

A FLY IS SEEN LANDING IN THE EYE OF THE
ELDERLY WOMAN THAT WAS KILLED BY THE LUNCH
BOX.

END MONTAGE.

INT. THE OFFICES OF BLOODTHIRST STREAMING - THE NEXT MORNING

BATEMAN is seen chugging a bottle of reflux
suppressant.

He drinks the entire bottle, makes an "Ahhh" sound as if completely refreshed, and throws the bottle over his shoulder.

A crashing sound is heard, but BATEMAN doesn't bother to look to see what broke.

> BATEMAN
> That should fight the anxiety for a couple of seconds.

BOGGINS looks at him, blank faced, as if this is completely normal behavior. He waits for him to respond.

> BOGGINS
> Ever tried alcohol?

BATEMAN continues talking as if he didn't hear BOGGINS.

> BATEMAN
> Well, we're the only two people left on Earth, BOGGINS. I guess no one wanted to give up their beer and popcorn in order to save their lives.

BOGGINS has a look of understanding flash over his face.

> BOGGINS
> I mean, have you ever tried beer and popcorn together, or even separately for that matter? It's the official snack of horrorphiles for a reason.

> Honestly, I don't blame 'em. I
> wouldn't give it up either.

BATEMAN is seen ripping up a piece of paper,
his resume, and throwing it over his shoulder,
like the bottle of reflux suppressant.

Strangely enough, another crashing sound is
heard.

Again, BATEMAN doesn't bother to see what
caused the sound.

> BATEMAN
> A lot of good my resume will do me
> now. You know, I labored over this
> thing and sweated it out and dreamed
> about all that would be on it since
> I was 10 years old!

> BOGGINS
> (interrupting him)
> (continued)
> That's a lot of wasted time! Think
> of all the movies you could've been
> watching!
>
> Now, in this situation, I would
> recommend the 1971 giallo film, THEY
> KILLED ME AT MY JOB, NOW I KILL THEM
> WHERE THEY SLEEP! from 1968: the
> year GEORGE ROMERO released the
> single greatest zombie film ever
> made, NIGHT OF THE LIVING DEAD!
>
> Now…

BATEMAN acts as if he doesn't hear BOGGINS.

BATEMAN
(interrupting BOGGINS)
What will I do? This company of
mine, one I built from the ground up
with my father's hard earned money,
is as good as gone.

Plus, nobody is left alive. I think
I said that already, but I'm tired.
I'm so damned tired. I think I said
that already, too.

Anyways, I guess we're out of a job.

BOGGINS
(cheerily)
Lovely. I always wanted a little
free time. I've been doing this
movie critic thing since the late
1950's, when drive-ins were at
their peak and the B-movie was at
its cheapest and most glorious.

BATEMAN
What are you going to do now?

BOGGINS
Some would say "I'm going to go to
DISNEYLAND", but I'm going to say,
just as enthusiastically, "I'm going
to go fishin'". Just like I used to
do as a youngin' off the waters of
The Louisiana River.

BATEMAN
We're the only two people left in
the world and you still are going to

bore me to death with your long-
winded diatribes, aren't you? Why
don't I put you back on air until
the four horsemen and the apocalypse
both come?

I might as well go eat some popcorn
and drink some beer myself.

        BOGGINS
Oh, I'm planning on doing just that!
I recommend you do the same. It's
the perfect treat. "Nature's candy",
as my old dad used to always say.

You see, The Louisiana River is
known for its bass fishing and…

BATEMAN HAS A "DEAR GOD, GET ME OUT OF HERE"
LOOK ON HIS FACE THAT FLASHES ON-SCREEN.

BOGGINS puts his arm across BATEMAN's back in
a way that suggests that they are two old
friends with all the time in the world to chat
about all things great and small.

The two slowly walk off screen with BOGGINS
talking non-stop, as if he doesn't notice the
look on BATEMAN's face.

FADE OUT.

PAR FOR THE COURSE

FADE IN:

INT. JACKSON OLIVER'S GARAGE- PRESENT- DAY

Thirty-nine-year-old loner JACKSON OLIVER, dressed in a gray alien suit, is hunched over a UFO he has been making for the past seventeen years in his garage. He, in case he ever got caught working on his UFO, looks like a solitary alien quickly stopping by Earth to repair his craft before journeying back through the stars. Hence, his deliberate attire. He figures that even if he doesn't get caught in his current fashion, the idea is amusing enough to him to be worth the effort alone.

With a welding torch that is mid-flame in his hand, he pauses. Staring at the television he long regretted putting in his garage to watch while he was working on his secret UFO project, he flips the gray alien mask off. He places it on the top of his head.

JACKSON listens to the news report.

> FEMALE NEWS ANCHOR
> (O.S.)
> …And sources say that The Pentagon is denying that the recently made public UFO reports have no credibility…

JACKSON OLIVER, long used to government denial of these sorts, grimaces.

                    JACKSON
            (to the FEMALE NEWS ANCHOR)
        Mmmmhmmm. Par for the course.

JACKSON goes back to working on his UFO for a
moment.

The same FEMALE NEWS ANCHOR changes the
subject to a political story.

                FEMALE NEWS ANCHOR
                (O.S.)
            In political news, a new scandal has
            challenged the Republican
            Presidential candidate…

JACKSON, with a look that can best be
described as "unsurprised" and "sick of it
all", changes the channel.

                FEMALE ANNOUNCER
                (O.S.)
            Next on *Remake of a Remake: The
            Sequel*…

JACKSON changes the channel again as the
"unsurprised" look turns even more angry and
disgusted with everything about modern day
humanity.

A MALE ANNOUNCER is heard.

                MALE ANNOUNCER
                (continued)
                (O.S.)
            …And the latest twelve-hour super-
            hero film to gross a billion dollars

in under twenty-four hours in pre-
sale tickets alone is…

JACKSON grunts, clenches his teeth,and changes
the channel.

> MALE ANNOUNCER 2
> (O.S.)
> …And the younger generation says
> they are offended by….

JACKSON grunts again, clenches his teeth
harder, and changes the channel.

> MALE ANNOUNCER 2
> (O.S.)
> …And the older generation says they
> are offended by…

JACKSON grunts again, bites down on his lips
to stop from crying out at hearing the same
news bits and society repeating the same
cycles over and over again, and changes the
channel.

> FEMALE ANNOUNCER 2
> (O.S.)
> …Again proving that if you were born
> rich you can say or do anything and
> get away with it…

JACKSON scrunches his face and shoulders in a
way that says this is an obvious statement. It
also says that he is just as unsurprised and
sick of statements like these as he is
everything else he is hearing today on
television.

                    JACKSON
               (to FEMALE ANNOUNCER 2)
          Thank you, Captain Obvious.

JACKSON turns the volume off on the tele-
vision, flips back on his gray alien mask like
a welder who is such a seasoned professional
that he can put on his welding hat in one
fluid motion before going back to work, and
quietly starts to labor on his UFO again.

In the midst of this toil, he continually
looks up from his work to see if the news will
break soon with what he calls "The Big
Announcement", which he has been waiting
seventeen years to hear.

CONTINUOUS SHOT:

JACKSON WORKING ON THE UFO WHILE A NARRATION
OF HIS THOUGHTS ARE HEARD OFF-SCREEN.

                    JACKSON
               (O.S.)
          I would say, "You probably want to
          know how I got like this" but, being
          alive now and a fellow active member
          in our current society, I am going
          to take a leap of faith and assume
          that you already understand in some
          way, shape, or form.

               (continued)
          So, what I will say instead is that
          my greatest fear as a young child
          used to be being taken from my room

and abducted and experimented on by
aliens. Nowadays, I welcome the
vacation.

There is even the newfound hope
welling within me that maybe they
will take me along with them, if
they ever do come, and I can be
their intergalactic pet and, in so
doing, I can go on nutty space ad-
ventures with them to other planets
and galaxies. Hell, I'd be happy to
have lunch with them while they are
on break from punching the clock at
their own daily grind at THE INTER-
GALACTIC DINER and being promptly
dropped off back home before they
clock back in for work.

Needless to say, and as showcased
previously with my recent channel-
surfing exploits, I'm fed up with
the repetitive cycles of humanity.
For example, the endless seething
political furies cast from one side
to the other.

I'm equally fed up with the name
calling that stems from said fury.

I'm also fed up with the way it
makes one side feel like they are
superior to the other because they
feel the way they do.

What is even worse, and possibly
even more childish, is the belief
that since the other side doesn't

adhere to this point of view 100% that it means that they are subject to being called and accused of the most grotesque things imaginable. In so doing, any relevant stereotype derived from said accusation can be hurled their way.

I almost find this last statement humorous because neither political side, and I say this fully knowing that there is a third option that just hasn't gained enough heft yet to be considered in the same league as the two main political options, seems to realize that this is exactly what those in higher positions of power want us to do. They want us to claw each other's eyes out over petty things so that we never realize how much we can change the world for the better if we all unite as one and put these petty grievances, the symbolic mountain built from the human molehill, aside.

Worst and most painful of all, I've seen certain authors I've long looked up to for what I thought was compassion, intelligence, and relatable "average Joe" demeanor fall victim to this "My side is the right side and anyone who disagrees is worthy of being called names and generally ridiculed in any way I see fit on social media" mentality. What these individuals in question don't understand is that by engaging in these types of actions they are no better than the erroneous individuals they think they are calling out.

It also presents them as the literary equivalent of schoolyard bullies. In short, it doesn't speak well of their character, whether you agree with these individuals or not. And character still matters. Possibly more now than ever before.

Plus, it makes your online conversations dull and one-sided because you (a) never present differing evidence from your opinion and (b) you never have any variety in subject matter in this regard.

It's made me lose respect for so many people that have inspired me to keep writing throughout the years.

We could also get into the argument of separating the author from their work and simply appreciating their material here. But, as a writer myself, I know that everything one writes contains a bit of the soul of the author. Thus, the two are inseparable.

In short, it's a pattern that's made me lose respect for so many people that have inspired me to keep writing throughout the years. I guess this proves the old adage of "Never meet your heroes" correct in some capacity.

This pattern is one I've noticed more frequently over the seventeen years since I officially said "I'm done with this shit" and decided to go online and study UFO reports to guess how they are built and, in so doing, do my best estimate on how to make me a Starman and get the ever-loving hell outta here.

Speaking of how I put this craft together, many of the reports said that the technologies and metals used in putting together the craft are non-existent on Earth. Well, I did my best to improvise.

This means that the chances that my craft will end up being an immobile hunk of metal are great, but who knows. Maybe I will have some luck. Maybe "The Big Announcement", a news report which says aliens have landed and are going to take willing captives aboard their ships or flatout annihilate us all, will be made in the meantime and all this will be null and void.

Knowing my luck, it won't. But, in case you were wondering why I even bother watching television at all,

when it just consists of short-lived
programs and half-baked ideas meant
to cater to the lowest common de-
nominator, there is your answer.

So, yeah, I put away most of a
weekly paycheck every month for
materials for this project that
probably won't pan out. I'd put more
money into the project if I wasn't a
victim of crippling and ever-growing
mortgage inflation rates. But, this
is a comedy. So, let's keep it
light. Aiight?

Anyways, the creation of this craft
gives my mind and body something to
do other than sit and stress over
every miniscule detail that isn't in
my capacity to change, like what
will The President of the United
States say now that will
collectively embarrass us and cause
potential nuclear fallout.

But, hey, what the hell do I know?
I'm just some unmarried dude with no
kids who has, at least in the eyes
of society, "wasted his life away
working in frozen food warehouses
for nearly two decades".

On that note, that is how I know
that even if the UFO doesn't fly or
work at all when all is said and
done I can at least have something
to show, a funny knick knack and a

unique creation, for my efforts.
It's the artist in me. That, in
itself, will make this all worth-
while.

See, that time I spent physically
working in the above-mentioned
warehouses, I would mentally be free
to compose poems and prose which I
would memorize and feverishly
scribble down on my lunch break.
This effort has resulted in me
publishing nearly two hundred works
which, again with my luck, haven't
made me a cent richer, wiser, or put
any real weight on my name as an
artist.

But, I digress kiddos, because, hey,
this is a comedy. Let's keep it
light. Aiight?

END CONTINUOUS SHOT.

JACKSON looks up to the television in his
garage. He stops working and tosses his gray
alien mask up to the top of his head again so
he can see the news. A look of delight
overtakes his countenance.

JACKSON grabs the remote and turns up the
volume.

                FEMALE ANCHOR 3
              (continued)
                (O.S.)
        …The pentagon is now going back on
        their earlier remarks as sightings

of giant, cigar-shaped craft have
been spotted all over the world.

                    JACKSON
               (delighted, to himself)
               (continued)
          I knew it! I knew you existed! I
          knew you'd come for me! And right in
          time to call out The Pentagon on
          their bullshit! This is beautiful!
          Just beautiful!

JACKSON abandons his work and stumbles dazedly
to the television.

                    FEMALE ANCHOR 3
               (O.S.)
          …The Pentagon is saying that there
          is no time left. They apologize for
          keeping America in the dark about
          extraterrestrials and wish for
          everyone to peacefully welcome these
          beings onto our planet in a way that
          proves our Core American values and
          overall humanity.

A blinding light comes out from the tiny
windows in JACKSON's garage.

He runs up to the windows, in hopes that the
light belongs to extraterrestrials landing
nearby to take him away from Earth, and sees a
long lineup of cars rear-ending one another as
neighbors who have recently heard the news try
to escape.

VARIOUS NEIGHBORS ARE SEEN FROM JACKSON'S
PERSPECTIVE ROLLING DOWN THEIR WINDOWS,

CURSING AT ONE ANOTHER, FIGHTING, AND TRYING
TO MANEUVER THEIR ALREADY MANGLED CARS TO BOB
AND WEAVE THROUGH THE TRAFFIC BY CRASHING INTO
EVERYONE AND EVERYTHING THEY CAN TO DO SO.

JACKSON, accustomed to this type of behavior
from everyone around him, looks up peacefully
as a blinding light fills his eyes.

He smiles and waves at the craft.

THE SHAPE OF SEVERAL UFOS HOVERING ARE SPIED
OVERHEAD.

JACKSON runs over to the garage door panel. He
hits the button to open the garage. It doesn't
work.

                    JACKSON
              (laughing to himself)
          Fate wouldn't have it any other way.

JACKSON runs over to the craft. He puts a key
marked GET ME OUTTA HERE into the door which
surrounds the ship. He watches as it reveals
the solitary panel and seat inside.

                    JACKSON
              (continued)
                (speaking lovingly to his
                craft)
          I sure hope you're ready, old girl.
          I know I am.

JACKSON jumps into the cockpit of the craft,
hits a button, and watches as the surrounding

doors close around him. His smile is so broad
it looks as if it may extend past his own
face.

Sounds of horns honking, name calling, and
other forms of loud, violent noise are still
heard outside.

>   JACKSON
>   (continued)
>   While the world was planning which
>   degree they would get or which job
>   they would widdle the woefully few
>   years of their lives left at after
>   the one they have now, as if that is
>   all man can aspire to do, I, unlike
>   the rest of the world, was planning
>   and waiting for this day.
>
>   Now, let's see if all that waiting
>   and planning has paid off.

JACKSON closes his eyes, throws his gray alien
mask back on, and turns the keys.

The engine of the craft sounds like it is
struggling to start.

JACKSON, eyes still closed, turns the key to
the OFF position. He waits a moment, turns the
key to ON again, and cries out in ecstasy as
the seat underneath him rumbles, the elec-
tronic navigation devices around him come to
life, and the fuel gauge goes from E to F.

JACKSON wipes away a solitary tear of joy from
his eye.

                    JACKSON
               (screaming in ecstasy)
            I did it! I did it!

JACKSON, planning on plowing through the
garage door with his craft since it wont open
and driving out from the skies to meet the
craft from his driveway, suddenly stops what
he is doing.

He turns up the volume from the television
with a button on his panel. FEMALE ANCHOR 3 is
heard from inside the craft.

                    FEMALE ANCHOR 3
               (O.S.)
            The Pentagon takes back what they
            said three minutes ago and they now
            wave the reports of the craft off as
            "mass hysteria" brought upon by "too
            much television watching" as reports
            arrive that the extraterrestrial
            ships were just going over the Earth
            to another destination.

                    JACKSON
               (to himself)
            They didn't think we were worthy of
            saving! They didn't have any faith
            in us!

            Maybe they looked down on all the
            violence caused by the news of their
            arrival and knew that we aren't
            fully developed and mature enough as
            a species to meet with, exchange
            ideas, and be one with them.

Their arrival would also obliterate
the human-made religious systems
Earth has set in place.

It'd obliterate the fake hierarchies
of the rich and poor, laborers and
those who profit off the laborers
that have been in place since the
dawn of time. It'd be too much for
us. We'd have to start from scratch,
even if they didn't obliterate us or
take all of us aboard, somehow
either way.

A look of complete disappointment overcomes
JACKSON's features.

It disappears as he realizes that his
interstellar vehicle worked and, in turn,
still poses as a chance for him to leave
Earth.

                    JACKSON
               (with renewed hope, to himself)
                 (continued)
          Well, not every recent turn of
          events has been a disappointment of
          monumental proportions.

JACKSON flips his gray alien mask back on,
cuts off the voice of FEMALE ANCHOR 3 in mid-
speech, and turns the key that is in the
ignition to ON.

The UFO comes quickly to life and JACKSON
gasps in joy.

The moment this ecstasy comes to him it turns to his expected disappointment as everything turns off.

The smell of smoke and a look of fire comes from the wire paneling to the controls.

JACKSON watches in disbelief as the F turns to E in the gas gauge.

Trying to do so and not realizing it won't work until he has tried it, the doors of the UFO don't come open either. This is because they are electrically controlled and connected to the wiring that has malfunctioned and is currently on fire.

JACKSON closes his eyes.

He listens to the shouting still coming from outside.

He looks around at everything wrong with his UFO wiring. A moment later he becomes visibly worried that he might not escape the UFO at all.

                    JACKSON
                (continued)
                    (whispering to himself)
            Par for the course.

The din outside grows louder and louder.

THE CAMERA PANS SLOWLY AWAY FROM THE CRAFT JACKSON IS INSIDE UNTIL HE TRULY LOOKS LIKE AN ALIEN WHO HAS LANDED IN SOMEONE'S GARAGE BY CHANCE.

EXT. THE ROAD JUST OUTSIDE JACKSON OLIVER'S GARAGE - SAME TIME

THE CAMERA PANS EVER-OUTWARD, TOWARDS THE HEAVENS, AS WE SEE HUMANS FIGHTING AND SHOUTING OVER THE TRAFFIC OUTSIDE.

THE HUMAN VOICES AND BODIES BECOME SMALLER AND LESS VISIBLE AS THE CAMERA GOES FURTHER OUT INTO THE HEAVENS. EVENTUALLY THE VOICES AREN'T SEEN OR HEARD AT ALL.

EXT. JUST OUTSIDE OF EARTH'S ATMOSPHERE - A MOMENT LATER

A UFO, exactly like that JACKSON made, hovers over Earth.

Broadcasts from the last few moments, announcing the aliens' arrival and going past Earth are heard coming from inside.

A GROUP OF GREY ALIENS ARE SPIED FROM AFAR WATCHING THEIR VERSION OF TELEVISION, THE SOURCE OF THE REPORTS, IN THEIR CRAFT.

The aliens, small and spindly shapes from where they are viewed, laugh and pound their fists on the control panels of their craft in laughter.

> ALIEN 1
> (laughing hysterically)
> These humans will never learn.

> ALIEN 2
> I'm sure they will just go back to
> their old ways tomorrow, even with

44

all they just learned as to what
lies beyond their cosmos, as if
nothing has happened at all.

            ALIEN 3
That's if they haven't already.

            ALIEN 4
Par for the course.

ALL FOUR ALIENS' laughter is heard as the UFO
quickly flies towards a planet with a big sign
sticking out from it labeled THE INTERGALACTIC
DINER.

                    FADE OUT.

THE HOUSE THAT NEEDED BLOOD

FADE IN:

INT. CARRINGTON HOUSE - NIGHT - 1859

The two current owners of CARRINGTON HOUSE in ROME, ITALY, forty-something LILITH and the suave and cynical BLACKWELL CARRINGTON, sit on opposite sides of a sleek, slender dining table in the kitchen of their castle. They listen to the pounding of the rain outside, watch the endless blankets of fog wrap around the house, and wordlessly lock eyes.

A single candle is in the middle of the table.

LILITH and BLACKWELL look at it. The candle extinguishes as a gust of angry wind rushes by. It sends goosebumps up their flesh.

> BLACKWELL
> (looking away from LILITH)
> That was another warning. The house needs blood, LILITH. What are we going to do?

> LILITH
> (speaking softly)
> We have to feed it, my love.

> BLACKWELL
> How? We've already fed the house the blood of every villager in town! We've even given the home our own blood! We just have to admit that we are out of options.

LILITH
(angrily)
There are always more options,
BLACKWELL! We can open up the home
under the guise of a spot that gives
sanctuary to weary travelers. Once
they are asleep, say 3 a.m. every
night, we kill them and throw them
into the crack in the ground where
the mouth of the home resides; the
one right here by our feet!

BLACKWELL
I know that part of the agreement we
made with the specters of the
current owners, the AUGUSTINES, on
the night we signed the lease in
exchange for our immortality was
that the local police would remain
clueless as to what was going on
here. Yet, we have tried that avenue
many times over the centuries we've
been here! I just keep thinking that
someone is going to find us out!

LILITH
Oh, BLACKWELL! I'm so terrified!
What are we going to do?

BLACKWELL
We'll do what we always do: stick
with what we know works, the tried
and true methods, to get this house
the blood it needs. Thus, we can
stay on this plane of existence and
as far away from the realm of
judgment for our libertine deeds as
possible.

                    LILITH
          Being immortal will not make us
          permanently escape judgment. It will
          only prolong it.

LILITH pauses for a long moment. She watches
the rain hitting the window. Tears start
forming in her eyes. She reaches out for
BLACKWELL's hand, but he draws it away from
her.

                    LILITH
                 (continued)
          Oh, BLACKWELL, please come to my
          rescue! Don't you love me anymore?

                    BLACKWELL
                 (angrily)
          Of course I do, darling, I-I just
          need a solution.

                    LILITH
          We've had to feed the house five of
          our living and five of our stillborn
          children, dear! Don't you think
          we've offered this house every
          solution we have?

                    BLACKWELL
                 (shaking with rage, but trying to
                 look calm)
          Don't you think that weighs on me
          day and night, LILITH? Don't you
          think it interrupts my daydreams and
          gives me persistent nightmares? It's
          done so for a millennia!

LILITH tries to reach out for the hand of
BLACKWELL again. BLACKWELL pulls his hand
away.

>   LILITH
> Speaking of nightmares, the AUGUST-
> INES have begun to visit me at pre-
> cisely 3 a.m. for the past six
> nights in my dreams. You know what
> that means, BLACKWELL!

>   BLACKWELL
>   (speaking in a more sympathetic
>   tone)
> Of course I do, darling.

>   LILITH
> They're serious! They need the blood
> on the seventh day or else the line
> that is the house, that of the
> living and the dead, will crumble
> and overrun the home.
>
> That means, all the specters within
> this domicile will be released into
> the world! All the creatures of hell
> and the angels of heaven will be
> one! It will be armageddon! And you
> know who the first one of us to be
> judged will be!

BLACKWELL gets up from his chair. He puts his
arms around LILITH.

>   BLACKWELL
> You know I am a solitary man,
> LILITH. All I need is you in this

world. Together we will make sure
that doesn't happen!

LILITH is crying. Her nerves have played upon
her too greatly at the thought of armageddon
being unleashed.

A SINGLE TEAR ROLLS DOWN THE RIGHT EYE OF
LILITH AS SHE LOOKS UP AT BLACKWELL.

LILITH is about to say something to BLACKWELL
when a loud rhapsodic knocking is heard
somewhere in the castle.

LILITH gasps. She covers her mouth to conceal
a scream pressing against her lips.

LILITH and BLACKWELL look towards the source
of the sound.

                    LILITH
          (clutching tighter to BLACKWELL)
          It's too much! It's all too much!
          They are going to put me back into
          one of those homes for the mad if
          this goes on too much longer!

          Oh, BLACKWELL! Please do something!
          I can't take this madness a moment
          longer!

As soon as LILITH utters these words, an
extended flame, like that from a blowtorch,
shoots out from the still unlit candle on the
table on its own accord.

The sound of knocking gets louder and louder.

LILITH and BLACKWELL remain silent and
immobile.

The two begin to hiss, vampire teeth exposed,
at the sound.

> BLACKWELL
> It's our makers! They have come to
> reclaim their end of our bargain for
> immortality.

LILITH CLUTCHES ONTO A STAKE THAT WAS HIDDEN
IN HER BLUE DRESS.

> LILITH
> I've come prepared for battle. I
> trust you have, too, my love!

Before BLACKWELL can respond, the AUGUSTINES,
JUSTINE and CLINT, materialize in front of a
grand staircase. It is one which leads into
the kitchen area LILITH and BLACKWELL are now
sitting in.

LILITH stands up promptly in the presence of
the AUGUSTINES. She is about to say something,
but JUSTINE makes a single silent sweeping
motion with her left hand.

LILITH takes the stake she was holding and
stabs BLACKWELL in the heart.

BLACKWEll, teeth bared and eyes red, tries to
say something, but nothing comes out. He
reaches towards the stake in his chest to pull
it out, but has no luck.

AUGUSTINE snaps her fingers.

The curtains partially concealing the windows in the kitchen slide open. The heavy rain and fog turns into mid-summer sun, which filters through the window and burns BLACKWELL's corpse.

A single rat squeaks. It comes out from a corner off to the right.

Before LILITH can respond, thousands of rats are coming from all areas of the home.

Their chewing sounds are amplified to LILITH's ears as they eat the corpse of BLACKWELL.

> JUSTINE
> Feast, soldiers of the night! Feast, my lovelies! The time has come for LILITH and BLACKWELL to switch sides!

LILITH stands more erect and stares JUSTINE down in a fury.

> LILITH
> That's not what we agreed on!

JUSTINE makes a lifting motion as she continues to walk slowly, almost nonchalantly and free of the stress and worry LILITH so visibly exudes, towards LILITH.

CLINT stays in step with his wife, JUSTINE, the entire time. They both echo the same relaxed manner.

JUSTINE, still casually moving towards LILITH, points her finger at the stake in BLACKWELL's chest. It quickly removes itself from the area in which it was lodged, turns itself towards LILITH and stops for a brief moment, and flies into LILITH's chest.

With the impact of the stake in her chest, LILITH falls onto her knees.

LILITH's FLESH IS BURNING FROM THE SUNSHINE SPILLING INTO THE ROOM. SMALL FLAKES PEEL AWAY FROM HER FACE AS LILITH TRIES TO COVER HER EYES FROM THE LIGHT IN HER FINAL BREATH BEFORE DEATH.

LILITH falls dead to the ground.

The rats quickly, hungrily consume her body. The awful sound their eating makes is amplified as the AUGUSTINES, still carrying the bloody axes to the head which signified their own deaths many years ago in the same areas which the event originally occurred, arrive at LILITH's body. They watch her get eaten with the same sadistic smile spreading over their faces.

JUSTINE snaps her fingers.

The curtains cover part of the window. The sunshine turns to rain and fog.

>   JUSTINE
>   (to CLINT)
>   Finally, my love, the external
>   weather matches my internal one.

CLINT is about to say something, but JUSTINE
shuts him up before he can do so.

                    JUSTINE
                    (continued)
          Shush, my dearest. You know you
          aren't allowed to talk. You're just
          here to follow and obey my every
          command, like a good husband should
          do.

CLINT nods his head obediently. He looks at
the ground as she addresses him.

                    JUSTINE
                    (continued)
          Now, back to taking what was
          rightfully ours.

JUSTINE and CLINT sit where LILITH and
BLACKWELL were seated only a few moments ago.

JUSTINE points at the candle in the table,
which has again lost its flame.

The candle quickly lights by itself.

A familiar sound, that of the rhapsodic
knocking which signified the coming of the
AUGUSTINES, is heard.

Instinctively, JUSTINE looks down at the
corpse of LILITH. It has vanished.

JUSTINE squints in the direction of the din.

                    JUSTINE
               (continued, to the din)
          That malmsey-nose hornswoggler! I'm
          onto your games, LILITH! We were
          here long before you were! It's our
          right to take this house back!

LILITH and BLACKWELL appear side-by-side as
the pair descend the steps in the same
leisurely fashion the AUGUSTINES demonstrated
a few moments ago.

JUSTINE tries to say something, but LILITH
points to the kitchen floor near where LILITH
and BLACKWELL are seated.

                    LILITH
               (continued)
          Silence!We've heard enough of your
          lies! Where you once brought rats,
          we are bringing the demons of hell
          to take you down to your eternal
          resting place! The blood that will
          be spilled by the seventh day will
          not be ours, but your own!

LILITH, still coolly walking towards JUSTINE,
puts two fingers, one on each hand together,
and quickly pulls them apart. The ground
around where the AUGUSTINES are seated splits
open.

JUSTINE and CLINT rise from their seats.

LILITH points towards the AUGUSTINES' legs.
Their extremities crack and pull apart,
leaving their bodies to fall onto the floor.

Half-human and half-vampire hybrid creatures, the GOAZ, rise from beneath the cracks in the ground.

They ravenously pull JUSTINE and CLINT, who were made flesh when LILITH and BLACKWELL unwillingly gave up their mortal lives in exchange for the AUGUSTINES.

The GOAZ, ever-pulling themselves out from the cracks in hell that LILITH unleashed, show their vampire teeth as their human arms pull out the AUGUSTINES innards and consume them.

Meanwhile, the creatures feast on the AUGUSTINES' blood. Some of the blood goes down the cracks to hell.

A satisfied sound, reminiscent of the din that was made to signify the coming of the AUGUSTINES and the CARRINGTONS, emanates from the cracks to hell.

In unison, the GOAZ stop eating the innards and drinking blood and uniformly hiss. They turn to the CARRINGTONS, who have finally stopped moving and have lost their cocky demeanor.

> THE GOAZ
> (in unison)
> This sacrifice is not enough! You made us wait! Now it will take even more to satisfy our cravings.

> LILITH
> No! This isn't what we agreed on!

                    BLACKWELL
          The devil is a liar! We knew this,
          but still we made a deal with them
          anyway! Where is god? Why has she
          forsaken us?

With these words, the GOAZ, we are still
multiplying in numbers as they pull themselves
from the cracks of hell, attack the
CARRINGTONS.

The GOAZ rip them apart limb-by-limb and
drinks their blood.

All the while, the candle on the table blows
out and quickly lights itself in an act which
signifies that there is a new owner of
CARRINGTON HOUSE.

In an act which is as mocking of the
AUGUSTINES and CARRINGTONS as it is part of
the tradition for those who think they own the
castle this unholy war is being waged on, two
GOAZ, one with a queen's crown and one with a
king's crown, sit where JUSTINE and CLINT and
LILITH and BLACKWELL once sat at the table.
They hold hands and look down upon their
fellow GOAZ as they eat flesh and innards and
drink human blood. A smile spreads on the
faces of these two GOAZ, which showcase their
vampire teeth.

                    MALE GOAZ
          This gateway to hell from which we
          arrived will forever be open and,
          henceforth, the prophesied arma-
          geddon will be upon us! So it is

wished and so it will be! Here is my
first order as the new owner of GOAZ
HOUSE!

The sound of lightning crackles outside.
Thousands of rats begin to scurry out from
hidden crevices in the floor to join in the
GOAZ's unholy consumption. The rats' awful din
fills with cries of pain and an almost sexual
joy.

The FEMALE GOAZ looks at the rain storm
outside. She looks at the chaos around her and
smiles.

The FEMALE GOAZ clutches the hand of the MALE
GOAZ tighter. A look of marital joy ensnares
her features.

                    FEMALE GOAZ
          I love the rain. It suits me.

The MALE and FEMALE GOAZ let out a sound of
ecstasy as another bolt of lightning flashes
through the sky.

                    FADE OUT.

THE SOIL

FADE IN:

EXT. MONTELL DOMINIC'S BACKYARD - PRESENT - NIGHT

A BEARDED MAN, FORTY-FIVE-YEAR-OLD MONTELL DOMINIC, IS SPIED IN A LONG SHOT AS A SHADOWY SILHOUETTE.

MONTELL violently jabs once into the dirt of the backyard garden of his home with a handheld shovel.

Blood spills from where the tip of the shovel lands in the soil. The gore splashes against the tip of MONTELL's already dirty work boots.

MONTELL begins frantically digging in the soil.

While digging, MONTELL starts pulling out hearts, intestines, and other bloody, writhing innards from the garden soil.

HE tosses them over his shoulder, digging evermore frantically. It is as if he doesn't even notice what he is holding.

MONTELL puts his ear to the soil. He stops digging.

Faint voices from the soil progressively begin to get louder.

                    VOICE FROM THE SOIL 1
                    (O.S.)
               Kill them!

A raspier voice is heard after the more
feminine-sounding initial voice from the soil
stops its brief command.

                    VOICE FROM THE SOIL 2
                    (O.S.)
               Kill them all!

An even raspier voice, one which could be
described as "pure evil", comes from the third
and final VOICE FROM THE SOIL.

                    VOICE FROM THE SOIL 3
                    (O.S.)
               The dirt is your weapon! Use it to
               kill them so that you can ensure
               that they will be with you in the
               afterlife!

                    MONTELL
                    (angrily)
               Never!

MONTELL backs up. He tries to get away from
the soil. Regardless, a hand reaches down from
where the voices were coming from and pulls
him even closer to the soil, in an attempt to
force MONTELL to listen to its demands.

MONTELL tightens his fist around the handheld
shovel. He is going to plunge it into the soil
in hopes of killing the source of the wicked
voices.

As if reading MONTELL's mind, the hand from
the soil grabs the hand with the shovel,
twists it all the way around, and, as bones
crack and MONTELL's hand goes limp, he drops
the shovel.

THE HAND uses this distraction to pull MONTELL
underneath the soil.

Title card appears: **THE SOIL**

**EXT. THE BACKYARD OF MONTELL DOMINIC'S HOME -
MINUTES LATER**

Another hand, eerily similar to the one that
pulled MONTELL in previously, suddenly reaches
out of the soil.

It lingers, as if dead, for a moment.

AFTER THE INITIAL PAUSE, THE ARM BEHIND THE
HAND IS SEEN.

Another hand and arms immediately reach-out
from beside the other arm.

THE EXTREMITIES push up on the grass until

MONTELL's corpse-like, maggot-ridden body slowly elevates from the soil.

INT. MONTELL DOMINIC'S HOME - MINUTES LATER

Ominous, rhythmic knocks come from outside the DOMINIC home.

MONTELL's wife, ATHENA, dressed in her silky pajamas and slippers with her hair in curlers, rushes to the door.

ATHENA looks through the sliding glass door by opening up the closed curtains and sees MONTELL.

A look of worry comes over her face and she furrows her brow.

She throws open the door, and is about to ask what he is doing in the backyard covered in dirt at 3 in the morning. Before she could say anything, MONTELL's arm, bloody and oozing white puss, pulls her head through the sliding glass door.

She tries to scream, but as soon as her mouth opens it is filled with the soil.

She gags. After a quick battle with trying to open her mouth and failing to do so, she chokes and dies.

MONTELL, in an unusual bout of strength for
someone with his slightly overweight frame,
hurls her into the soil.

She quickly and completely sinks into it in no
time.

MONTELL sees his son, AARON, staring at him
through his window to the right of where he is
standing.

                    MONTELL
          Oh, son! Daddy's home!

MONTELL menacingly walks, cooly and
confidently, to the door that is hanging wide
open.

He stares up at the door to AARON's room.

CLOSE-UP ON A PATCH OF DIRT IN MONTELL'S RIGHT
FIST.

BEGIN MONTAGE:

AARON, seeing that his dad is now in the
house, tries to escape by opening his window.

MONTELL's shadow looms over him as AARON tries
to escape.

MONTELL catches AARON as he tries to jump out
the window.

MONTELL shoves dirt down AARON's throat.

MONTELL throws AARON in the soil.

MONTELL cocks his head after throwing AARON in the soil. The three VOICES FROM THE SOIL congratulate him.

> VOICES FROM THE SOIL
> (in unison)
> You have pleased us! Rest now!

MONTELL drops to the soil with his head resting on the patch of dirt where he had been feverishly digging mere minutes ago.

DREAM SEQUENCE:

INT. MONTELL DOMINIC'S BACKYARD - NIGHT

A SILENT SHOT OF MONTELL THROWING HIS WIFE AND SON'S BODIES IN THE SOIL.

Suddenly, something immense hits the ground with a violent thud near his feet.

It's AARON's body.

MONTELL, with tears of regret silently streaming down his eyes, reaches for his son.

MONTELL embraces AARON.

MONTELL mouths words of apology, but it is cut off by an ear-splitting din.

Another quick, violent thud, this one followed by the sound of a gory splat, as ATHENA's body rains down from the sky. It lands by MONTELL's feet right next to where AARON landed.

Before MONTELL can react, hundreds of variations of AARON and ATHENA's bodies are hitting the ground from the sky with a gory splat.

A CLOSE-UP SHOT AS ONE LANDS AND SPLASHES ITS GORY REMAINS ONTO THE CAMERA.

After a period of time, this inexplicable event stops.

MONTELL's face is a mixture of grief, regret, fear, and sorrow as his head instinctively turns to the garden soil that is now a middle-of-the-backyard graveyard.

MONTELL's face becomes even more horrified as his eyes move from left to right. This is done without his head turning from the soil graveyard.

All of the bodies that had just rained from the sky have disappeared.

Suddenly, two pairs of arms reach out from the soil graveyard.

The now demonic inflections of AARON and ATHENA stem from the soil.

> AARON, ATHENA
> (in unison)
> It is so empty here without you! You sent us here, yet you aren't man enough to come join us!

MONTELL looks down and sees the body of AARON still in his arms.

AARON's black eyes open. He hisses like a snake and bites MONTELL's neck.

The bite pulls gory strands of flesh from the entry point as blood completely covers AARON's face.

> AARON
> (in MONTELL's arms, chanting)
> Join us! Join us! Join us!

Soon this chant rises from the soil graveyard.

> AARON, ATHENA
> (from the soil, in demonic tones)
> Join us! Join us! Join us!

An unexpected voice is heard addressing
MONTELL from nowhere in particular.

                    STRANGE VOICE
             You will wake now!

End dream sequence.

INT. MONTELL DOMINIC'S BEDROOM - MOMENTS LATER

MONTELL opens his eyes to find himself inches
away from a wall that wraps around the
circumference of his bedroom.

MONTELL's eyes enlarge. He shrieks as he sees
two pairs of dirty and dismembered arms, which
he realizes are those of the family members he
just killed, reaching out of the wall. They
are just a few inches from his face.

The fingers flex and barely touch his cheek.

MONTELL screams, backs up, hits his writing
desk, and jumps to his feet.

MONTELL screams again as he spins around the
room.

Dismembered body parts of all types, all of
which belong to his beloved slain family
members, are writhing in the walls. They also
reach-out towards him.

MONTELL backs up from a set of arms, one which he recognizes as that of his son, grabbing a piece of the shirt on his right shoulder.

The arms tear a patch off his shirt, but MONTELL spins around, screams, and backs up onto a table.

MONTELL notices that his scream causes all the body parts to momentarily stop their dance on the walls.

With this in mind, he lets out one long scream.

While doing this, with the veins branching out from MONTELL's neck like roots in a tree and his head bouncing in front of and behind him to make sure the body parts have stopped their rhythmic movements, he runs to the door in hopes of escape.

Inches away from the door, MONTELL's arm is about to turn the knob on the entryway, the door violently swings open by itself.

MONTELL's eyes begin to widen. His extended scream turns more guttural as he sees into the next room, his kitchen, where arms are stuck into the kitchen sink, reaching out and spewing blood all over the room. The grinder

underneath the kitchen sink is heard running
and making an ear-splitting sound as it sprays
the remains everywhere.

MONTELL backs up into his bedroom. He is too
startled to scream. He sees dissected ears,
eyes, and limbs forming a neat line throughout
the kitchen.

MONTELL turns his head to a sound outside his
house.

Through the bedroom window, which gives him a
perfect view from where he is standing, he
sees his wife and son emerge in tandem next to
each other from the soil graveyard.
Vines are sprouting from and twisting around
their arms, necks, ears, and legs.

ATHENA opens her mouth to speak. As she does
so, a vine pokes out and wraps around her
lips.

                    ATHENA
          (in a demonic voice so loud it
          makes the walls shake inside the
          bedroom MONTELL is in)
          The punishment for your crime of
          death is your death!

MONTELL blinks, shocked and dumbfounded, as
ATHENA and AARON start slowly walking towards

the house with their arms out in typical
zombie fashion.

MONTELL feels further revulsion as he sees
dirt in their fists and, remembering his
crimes onto them, knows that this image is
meant to be seen. Therefore, he knows what his
family members are intending to do to him.

As ATHENA and AARON step away from the grave,
two more exact copies of ATHENA and AARON
suddenly appear from the grave.

They follow several feet behind the original
versions of ATHENA and AARON. They also have
dirt in their fists.

Soon another copy of the two suddenly appear
from the grave. Immediately afterwards,
another pair of the duo emerges.

MONTELL wordlessly, and in utter disbelief,
shakes his head 'no'.

Soon all of the copies of ATHENA and AARON
start chanting what ATHENA first said only
moments ago.

                    ALL ATHENA, AARON COPIES
                  (chanting in unison)
                The punishment for your crime of
                death is your death!

As the chant continues, a pair of hands grab
MONTELL by the neck.

MONTELL tries to break free and fails to do
so.

From his peripheral vision, he can see that
what is causing his immobility is a pair of
arms reaching frenziedly from the wall.

He realizes he has stopped screaming.

Beginning to scream again, a hand pulls his
mouth open and cuts off the yell.

It is his wife, ATHENA.

She shoves soil in his mouth until he gags.

MONTELL's eyes widen as he gags.

ATHENA keeps shoving the soil into his mouth.

From the soil inside his mouth, a vine grows.

The vine forms a dagger, big enough for
MONTELL to see, that wraps around his throat
and strangles him.

AARON rips open his chest. He haphazardly
throws his organs around the room like MONTELL

did with the innards growing from the soil at the commencement of this nightmare.

As the chanting grows louder and louder, this time the body parts from the kitchen and bedroom are joining in on the chant and the copies of AARON and ATHENA are entering the room and doing the same, AARON puts dirt in the hole in MONTELL's chest.

AARON pulls out a miniature version of MONTELL from MONTELL's open chest. He quickly smashes it onto the floor.

>   AARON
>   Oh, soil; giver of life, Giver of
>   destruction— Grief is malformed; An
>   internal malfunction Known, sensed A
>   stone Upon waters, daughters A mind
>   Born To be Dispensed.

By the time AARON has finished his poetic chant, the copies of AARON and ATHENA are pulling him apart, shoving soil in his wounds, pulling out miniature versions of MONTELL, and destroying them in tandem.

In his dying moments, MONTELL tries to apologize to his son but can't speak because of the vine ever-tightening around his throat.

Instead, MONTELL gently closes his eyes.

DARKNESS FADES OVER THE SCREEN AS MONTELL
LOSES SIGHT.

                    AARON
                    (O.S.)
          This is your purgatory; a cycle you
          will repeat forever for your
          actions! This is the power of the
          soil. This is the power of grief!

THE CAMERA LINGERS IN DARKNESS AS THESE WORDS
ARE HEARD BEING CHANTED BY ALL THE BODY PARTS
AND ATHENA AND AARON COPIES.

                    FADE OUT.

CHECK-IN TIME FOR THE CREATURES AT THE

THORNTON INN

"No, I killed every one of you years ago," forty-year-old Marilyn Thornton screamed at the bathroom mirror of suite seventy-two of The Thornton Inn. As if on cue with her raging sentiments, the mirror suddenly split in half. In the same span, it swelled with hauntingly familiar images of bloodthirsty beasts. "Our agreement was that if I wiped you all out before either one of you killed me then you would let me rest! I have a family now! I can't keep doing this!"

"Ah, yes, my dear," the pig masked slasher who initiated Marilyn's fate as a final girl one Halloween night twenty-five years ago, The Necker, ominously whispered as he appeared behind Marilyn, "But, you've overlooked two things. One, our patience. We have all the time in the world to wait and to plot. And, two, the power of the multiverse from which we come. This being, of course, resurrection. You can kill us as many times as you want, Marilyn. But, we are still here. You have to find the one thing that will make all of our hearts, or the organs that we have in place of what you humans call such a foolish impetus, collectively stop. And you must do it throughout the multiverse of hell."

The lights flashed off. When they immediately went back on, Marilyn gasped as The Necker held his blade to her throat. The sound of a drain dissolving the watery contents within interrupted them. Solus the Amphibian, a six-foot human and frog hybrid reminiscent of the Gill-man from the 1954 horror classic *Creature from the Black Lagoon*, pulled the shower curtain back, a la Norman Bates in Alfred Hitchcock's *Psycho,* and showcased his green, pockmarked skin and razor-like dorsal fin in the mirror before Marilyn. His smell, which was more like rancid milk than fish, hit Marilyn's nostrils as soon as the shower curtain parted.

"I drowned you in the Amazon," Marilyn hissed at Solus as he began to slither soundlessly out of the shower and wrap himself around her feet until extreme claustrophobia overtook her. Marilyn could almost feel Solus effortlessly crushing her like a python.

"Again, you ignore what our good pal The Necker said. We aren't technically dead. You failed. Therefore, our verbal contract is still valid. But, we do have a proposition for you."

The lights went out again. Once they illuminated the scene once more, Marilyn's eyes widened. She wanted to scream, but before she could open her mouth The Necker put his machete so close to her throat that the chilly tip began to draw blood. What Marilyn saw was that the images in the ruptured fragments of the mirror were gone. They were replaced with oozing blood.

"Jeremy, the ghost of the boy I freed from being stuck forever in an ancient version of this home in the multiverse of hell, I assume that is you."

The lights went out and back on once more. That was Marilyn and Jeremy's way of communicating with one another when she was trying to free him over a decade ago. One flicker of the lights meant "yes". Two flickers of the lights meant "no".

"I tried to free you! You should be on my side," Marilyn cried out in anger.

"We have both of your children," The Necker whispered with a raspy inflection in her ear. Briefly, she thought she heard their cries for her echo through the floor beneath her, which was the gate to the multiverse.

Marilyn closed her eyes. She remembered what she had in the drawer a few inches from her fingers in case her past came back to haunt her like this one day. But, she knew she couldn't pull the drawer open and hit the button on the blood crystal to make their "hearts", for lack of a better word, explode and get these bloodthirsty brutes out of her life forever in time.

"Yes," Solus said, "We will make you an offer."

"Never," Marilyn screamed so loudly that she felt the veins branch out in her neck.

"We will take them to the multiverse of hell with us and make them our personal errand girls. Simply put, they will be our eternal slaves. In doing so, you can have peace. You can have your quaint little inn in the heart of Mineral Ridge, Ohio. You can have your fall weather. You can have whatever you want. We can even reach our talons into your brain through your left eardrum and erase any lingering maternal instinct you may have left in your body as well as any memories you have of your two dear daughters. We can do the same with any recollections of us, the creatures that have haunted your daydreams and your nightmares for decades. Therefore, your insomnia will be cured. We can even make you fall in love, if that is your preference, so you won't be so lonely."

Marilyn's eyes were closed as she listened to this insidious tirade. She didn't know if it was her imagination or actually occurring right before her, but in that instant she felt a finger-like hook shape fill her eardrum. She knew it was the werewolf, Dazeul, who had found her once again after she shot him with a silver bullet in a forest in the moon area of the multiverse of hell.

"*Your silence means that you are indecisive,*" the unmistakable voice of the gray alien Besbuz telepathically sounded in Marilyn's brain. "*How about we tell you what will happen if you don't let us have your children? Which, let's be honest, may not be a choice that is entirely yours to begin with. It may be a choice that was already made in one of the many dimensions of the multiverse and we are just giving you the impression of free will.*"

"*But, I digress,*" Besbuz continued. "*What will happen is that we will haunt this inn from the interior of the building itself to the woodlands you have conveniently located in the surrounding exterior of the property. We will kill every single person that has the misfortune of signing up to spend the night here.*"

"*Quickly,*" Besbuz went on, "*Rumors about you and about this place will circulate. Cops will come swarming in. You will be arrested and immediately sentenced to die by the hands of the state for murdering everyone who sets foot into the doors of The Thornton Inn. Your legacy will be that of a mass murderer.*"

"*And your two beautiful daughters, nine-year-old Callie and eleven-year-old Sophia,*" Besbuz further taunted. "*What will happen to*

*them? They won't be able to keep a job because
everyone in town will think that they are just
like their dear old mommy. They will be given
psyche tests and quickly institutionalized.
The stigma of you as a murderer will carry on
with all your future relatives until the
family name completely dies out from
generations of isolation. Now, you don't want
all that weighing on your tiny, insignificant
conscience. Do you?"*

"Mommy," a terrified cry from below
Marilyn's feet exploded, which she instantly
recognized as the voices of both of her
daughters, "It's got us wrapped up in its web!
It's killing us, mommy!"

"*Spectros*," Marilyn thought as visions of
the fifty-foot spider with one hundred eyes,
one she killed by setting her and her eggs on
fire in a dimension of the multiverse of hell
which was essentially a giant barn, feeding
her children to her spiderlings exploded in
her mind.

Without thinking, Marilyn threw the
drawer with the blood crystal open. But, the
crystal was gone. It was only after doing so
that she saw its shattered remains below her
feet. Somehow, either The Necker or Solus the
Amphibian had used the distraction of the
lights flashing on and off to open the drawer
and smash the crystal.

Suddenly, everything went quiet as the
early afternoon hours gave way to the
relentless darkness of midnight. The sound of
the windows in the dining area of the suite
violently throwing themselves open was heard
from where Marilyn was standing in the
attached bathroom.

She knew who was behind all this without even seeing or even receiving a clue as to who or what it may be. As a single bat flew from the living room onto Marilyn's shoulder, she knew the master of the multiverse of hell, the vampire Gavator, was the one who was behind this newfound din. This comprehension was only confirmed as Gavator wordlessly sank its mighty teeth into Marilyn's neck.

As the pinprick impression of the fangs went beneath her flesh, Marilyn felt zombie arms from the ground beneath her pulling her down. As the roaming, rendering mouths of the un-dead peeled Marilyn's flesh from the bone like chicken, she knew these henchmen of Gavator were just enacting the first bit of the pact Marilyn had made with her new master.

She had long understood that there was no way of defeating these beasts. Moreover, she also understood their ability to reactivate the cycles of resurrection until they got what they wanted from her, the final girl who would not die or give in to the demands from the creatures from the multiverse of hell. So, seeing this rendezvous that was playing itself out in front of her right now a decade ago, she made a pact with Gavator to make her immortal by biting her neck and making her become a vampire when these beasts finally came for her. That way, she could roam the multiverse of hell without worrying that the murderous fiends within its depths would slaughter her or wear her down to subservience.

Even though she had to sacrifice both her physical body and her soul to Gavator, she was aware, as the zombies pulled her near lifeless body down to hell and she saw an eyeball-filled skull looking back to her in the shattered mirror she was in the routine act of cleaning only a few minutes ago, that she would succeed in her quest to save both her children and her family's name.

It wasn't until Marilyn saw her corporeal self from outside of her body, like a ghost, cobwebbed, immobile, and pale as she clutched her copycat children that she realized Gavator was not going to make good on his end of the bargain.

Digging into her past experiences in the multiverse of hell, she became well aware of the memory of a similar situation involving a barn and Spectros. Hoping to replicate her earlier successes, she looked around and saw a torch hanging overhead. Even though Gavator was a master of mental illusions, and this could well be one, she soon became painfully cognizant of what she must do for the sake of her children's survival. But, first, she had to figure out how to take over her old body and move again.

A FUNERAL DIRGE PLAYS ITS GROOVE

Lights on.

The snarling beast comes from the portal—
A six-foot, pumpkin-necked immortal—
And takes my mother's head.

Lights off.

I was safe,
Even though someone else would soon be dead.

Lights on.

Another shapeshifter appears
From The Dimension of Shadows;
The Wormhole of Mirrors.

His presence is felt,
Eager talons on my elbows.

Lights off.

A wolf-like cry, a high-pitched howl
From somewhere near the kitchen window.

Lights on.

Blood dribbles down my neck in rivulets;
A crimson bow.
I spy my body hanging near my toes—
Thump-thump—

Banging slow.

Lights off.

A sudden flash of lightning, leaves.
The monster, Armageddon, is here.
I can't let him hear me breathe.
I can't gasp. I must fight my terrified tears.

But, I hear
Their telepathic taunts in my mental gears.

I search for the door to their dimension
Because, I have yet to mention,
The dark flashes are my only moment of safety.
My only chance to crawl out of the grave they
made for me.

Lights on.

There are two of them now.
The creatures are multiplying. How?
I have no time to ask.
All I know is their faces aren't there.
They are blank,
Spectral mirrors of my own despair.

My eyes hurt, senses tire from the task
Of searching to see where
They are.
Light comes from their open mouth like a star.

Mental pictures of the sinister sun

Exploding, undone;
A skeleton in the desert pounding a drum.

My soul, emotions become
Rigid, a childhood mask
Because I know they are
Coming for me.

I see them from the corner of my eye
(Even if I don't know why).

They circle quicker
With every momentary burst of light,
Every candle flicker,
Every new insight.

They inhale my misery, bite,
Intoxicated on the fluids of my fear.
Their fangs at my jugular like a flask.

Bloodthirsty, brutish, and ready
To render me externally—
A forceful surrender—
Contents of my veins spilling steadily
In a whir like a blender.

I'm the only
Member of my family
Left.

Lights off.

I run to the red-rimmed door
Levitating above the kitchen floor.

It's humming an ethereal tune
That compliments the current full moon,
The ambiance of this Halloween night,
The jackal's croon.

Lights on.

The razor-toothed entities,
Which smell cadaverous,
Their rotting flesh—
The decaying flowers of hell—
Satan's mermaids sacrificing fish
As they make promises to me I can't foretell.
My ears weep red, though covered,
A temporary bliss from this parallel.

Lights off.

Laughter from trick-or-treaters out past
curfew.

Lights on.

I have no idea what to do.

Lights off.

The clock strikes midnight and never moves.

Lights on.

A funeral dirge plays its groove.

THE ENIGMATIC TUFTS, LIKE TONGUES, MORPHED INTO MYSTIFIED MISTS WHICH MOTIONLESSLY LINGERED OVER THE COUNTRY FOR THIRTY YEARS

The enigmatic tufts, like tongues, morphed
into mystified mists
Which motionlessly lingered over the country
for thirty years.

No one questioned, like so many things, their
right to exist —
To hover, watch, in their amorphous forms, our
collective joys, fears.

But, I, keeping a journal that was hidden in
the cabinet of the mind,
Noted the changes, most indiscernible, to
mankind.

The switch of empathy seemed to liquify in my
fellow citizens,
An observation woven by even the least
attentive pushers of the pen.

Thus, a feeling of the surreal swirled audibly
from their voices, perspectives
And I simply wondered about unhappiness —
professions, electives.

And, in a throaty whisper, these beings became
more selective
In individuals, interactions. They were also
far more protective.

I pondered the mystified mists for decades,
Societal evolution like an autumn tree
withdrawing from the shade,

The fog-like sky, the eyeless observers and
their intentions,
And I became a key to another dimension —

One that I entered at will as an escape, a
coping mechanism,
A way of making sense of the humdrum prism,

Life, via creation. That is, until I looked
outside my writings,
Eternal echoes from the caverns of my psyche
on silent wings,

And the content, like those around me, became
Sadder, more withdrawn, insecure, filled with
shame.

It was a sensation communicated by an internal
burning
When my questions went unanswered

As the climate-changing shapes, like a dancer,
Tip-toed to dust; a melancholy signal of blue
skies returning.

Even in the aftermath, no one spoke of the
alterations which transpired.
And I, like all others, submitted my lingering
speculations to the fire.

*"This is how it is when we are confronted with
something we don't understand,"*
I quietly, naively thought.

And I believed my own lies, 'til a clutching
of a quill in my right hand
On a late August morning proved my hypothesis
was overwrought.

Soon, the mystified mists were restored, if
only for a day,
In an act of wish fulfillment, temporary love,
and inevitable decay.

Soon, the mystified mists reappeared
And I penned brilliant horrors under a glass-
less mirror.

Soon, the mystified mists became an expansion
of my brain,
A weathervane extending to spiritual,
metaphysical planes.

Soon, we were one.
I blotted out the stars. The mystified mists
blotted out the sun.

Yet, no one spoke of or ever did mention,
Even after I was long gone, my sudden arrival
or intention.

THE TALE OF ABBY GALE

Descended from a family of witches, Abby Gale
Was born with a broom in her hands, a snake's
tail,

And a cackling laugh that would make her
nannies say,
"I quit! This is too much for only ten pennies
a day!"

As an infant she could control the wind with a
twirl
Of her finger. She'd make it linger, whirl,

Knock off her daddy's straw hat with a loving
poke.
Still, this power, though fun, was no joke.

At eleven, her pranks turned frightening
As clouds hovered over her with their own
lightning.

Wherever she went, lunch trays would fly,
people would trip
As her trademark laugh escaped her lip.

As she got older, a high schooler,
She thought it would be much cooler

To harness her power into words, a book
That would act like a mental hook

Which would put audiences in a spell
With the words on the page, poems which did
tell

Her story, her side of things.
Thus, audiences of all ages grew wings

And possessed her abilities, glimpsed her mind
And this understanding did bind

More souls to pick up their own brooms,
Pens, see the beauty in the gloom,

And embrace their unique powers, creative
self.
Thus, more libraries offered special hexes, a
wealth

Of voices captured between pages on the shelf

And as more children embraced the broom, the
snake's tail
The legend of the birth of Abby Gale
Was no longer a horror story, but a love tale.

A SECRET HAUNTING

The library is haunted by the voices of
brilliant minds
That speak their tales, wisdom once a volume
is opened, the blinds

Put over their ageless lips unsealed
As the hush of the page unfolded allows them
to live again, feel

Their familiar sensations, heal
The hallowed nearby hallways with real

Knowledge, centuries of concealed
Intellect. So, in secrecy some find

Themselves compelled
To listen to, memorize, enact the spells

Put on the page, ghosts summoned from words
Which possesses the brain as soon as their
ancient story is heard.

These folks know that if you go
To the library on your own with a willing
heart in tow

Sometimes you'll even hear their voices
whisper, squeak
Like wheels on a table, and become inclined to
see them speak

From a ghostly corner, a spooky silhouette,
A bit of homework on proper etiquette.

And sometimes if you engage enough with a tale
The author's full form will mysteriously
prevail

And appear with a comforting pat on your
shoulder, a wise smirk
That makes you become obsessed, a newfound
quirk,

With conjuring them through their work.

THE LIBRARY OF SOULS: A WRITING PROMPT

A hundred years in the future, scientists, many of whom we would call 'mad', have assembled a place where the dying screams of long-deceased victims are collected. These cries, taken before the death of said victim, are noted to become physical things, small like a butterfly, when they are expelled from the lungs of the individual who once held them. These shrieks are jarred upon arrival. They call this high-tech morgue The Library of Souls.

It's a painfully quiet place where these silent screams wait to be put in a body. The body that is alive, but mimicking death, next to them. Here, the doctors go about their day in a detached, clinical fashion. Here, people pay money to gawk at these dying screams. Here, these merry guests take selfies with the jarred screams, the doctors, and even take said screams home for their own amusement.

ABOUT THE AUTHOR

Andrew Buckner is a multi award-winning screenwriter and filmmaker.

A noted poet, actor, author, critic, and experimental musician, he runs and writes for the review site AWordofDreams.com.

A Word of Dreams

The Library of Souls

Souls

A COLLECTION OF
TEN HORROR
SCRIPTS, TALES,
AND POEMS

Andrew Buckner